LOOK FOR ALL OF IGGY'S TRIUMPHS

The Best of Iggy

Iggy Is Better Than Ever

Iggy Is the Hero of Everything

Iggy the Legend

THE BEST OF IGGY

ANNIE BARROWS

ILLUSTRATED BY SAM RICKS

putnam

G. P. Putnam's Sons

G. P. PUTNAM'S SONS
An imprint of Penguin Random House LLC, New York

First published in the United States of America by G. P. Putnam's Sons,
an imprint of Penguin Random House LLC, 2020
First paperback edition published 2022

Visit us online at penguinrandomhouse.com

THE LIBRARY OF CONGRESS HAS CATALOGED THE HARDCOVER EDITION AS FOLLOWS:
Names: Barrows, Annie, author. | Ricks, Sam, illustrator.
Title: The best of Iggy / Annie Barrows; illustrated by Sam Ricks.
Description: New York: G. P. Putnam's Sons, [2020]
Summary: Relates three times that nine-year-old Iggy got into trouble,
two of which he does not regret and one for which he is very, very sorry.
Identifiers: LCCN 2018055049 (print) | LCCN 2018058772 (ebook)
ISBN 9781984813312 (ebook) | ISBN 9781984813305 (hardcover)
Subjects: | CYAC: Behavior—Fiction.
Classification: LCC PZ7.B27576 (ebook) | LCC PZ7.B27576 Bes 2020 (print)
| DDC [Fic]—dc23
LC record available at https://lccn.loc.gov/2018055049

Printed in the United States of America

ISBN 9781984813329

1 3 5 7 9 10 8 6 4 2

LSCH

Design by Marikka Tamura
Text set in New Century Schoolbook LT Std

For a certain person who shall be nameless,
with congratulations on not burning down the garage.
—A.B.

To Mom and Dad,
who survived a surprising number of Iggycidents.
—S.R.

CONTENTS

CHAPTER 1

THINGS
WE WISH
WE HADN'T DONE

All of us do things we wish we hadn't done. Sometimes, we say we wish we hadn't done a thing, when what we really wish is that we hadn't gotten in trouble for it. Other times, we wish we hadn't done quite as much of the thing as we did. But once in a while, not very often, we wish we had not done the thing at all. We wish it could be erased. We wish we had never thought of it. We wish we could go back in time and not do it.

But we can't.

Because we aren't magic.

This is not a book about magic.

This is a book about a boy named Iggy. (You probably want to know why he was named Iggy, but I'm talking about something else right now.) Iggy is what's called the *hero* of this book. Does that mean he's polite and nice and plays the cello and reads for at least half an hour before bedtime?

No.

Iggy is the hero of this book because he's the one who does the things in it. All the things he does (in this book) are bad. Every last one of them. It's really a shame you have to hear about such bad things, nice children like you. You would never do these things.

You say.

Do you remember the beginning of this book?

You should. It wasn't very long ago. Just in case you are paying no attention at all, here is a list:

THREE TYPES OF THINGS WE WISH WE HADN'T DONE

1. Things we say we wish we hadn't done, but actually just wish we hadn't gotten in trouble for
2. Things we wish we hadn't done quite as much as we did
3. Things we really, completely wish we hadn't done

You probably notice that this list goes from bad to worse. Number 1 is not so bad. We are a little sorry we did it, but still, it was fun. Number 2 is half bad. Maybe even less than half. It wasn't ever a good idea, but it wouldn't have been so bad if we hadn't gone too far. We're sorry about going too far. Number 3 is the worst. Completely bad. We feel awful when we think of it.

We're
very
very
sorry.

In this book, Iggy Frangi will do all three types of bad things. He will go through Numbers 1, 2, and 3. That's what this book is about: bad things Iggy did. You will also learn about an important idea called *extenuating circumstances*, but not right now.

Right now, I think it's time you met Iggy. He's in his room. He's going to be in his room for quite a while. He's going to get pretty bored. Some kids have computers or even TVs in their rooms, but not Iggy. Iggy's parents believe in screen-free kids.

Iggy has tried to explain that their lives would be better if they let him have a computer in his room, because then he'd be too busy to do anything bad. Their answer to this was too complicated to go into. Basically, they said, Forget it.

But now—Iggy. Here he is.

Yes, that's him. He's nine. He has brown hair.

He is lying facedown on his old, hairy rug.

He has to stay in his room until dinnertime. It's two thirty in the afternoon. That means he has four hours to go.

This is his punishment. Part of it, anyway. He is also getting no dessert for a week.

Plus no allowance next month.

Plus he has to write an apology letter. He is supposed to be writing it right now.

Poor Iggy.

Is he lying facedown on his rug, feeling bad about himself?

No.

Iggy is lying facedown on his rug, laughing.

CHAPTER 2

THE WONDERFUL BOY (NOT IGGY)

Iggy Frangi is laughing. He can't help it. He's held it in for a long time. He almost laughed way back that morning, when Jeremy Greerson came through the front door with his mom. Why? Because the kid was wearing a scarf. A scarf!

Of course, Iggy didn't laugh. Laughing would have been rude. Also unfair, because probably, Jeremy didn't *want* to wear a scarf. Probably, his mom made him.

Moms make you do stuff.

Iggy's mom, for example, made him hang out with Jeremy, because she was friends with Jeremy's mom. Why wasn't she friends with the moms of guys Iggy liked? Those moms seemed fine to Iggy. But no, she had to be friends with Mrs. Greerson. And Mrs. Greerson had to have Jeremy. And both of them had to come over for brunch.

At the front door, Iggy's older sister, Maribel, said, "Hi, Jeremy."

"Hi, Maribel," said Jeremy.

"Iggy?" said Iggy's mom. This meant, Say hi to Jeremy.

"Hi," said Iggy.

"Hi," said Jeremy.

"I like your scarf," said Maribel.

Iggy made a face.

"I do," she argued (with Iggy's face, because he hadn't said anything). "Jeremy's got style." Ever since she'd turned eleven, Maribel said things like this, about clothes. Iggy thought it was dumb.

Iggy didn't say it was dumb. Iggy said nothing. Nothing was nice, compared with the things he was thinking. But did Iggy get credit for being nice?

No. His mom gave Iggy the fish-eye. "Why don't you and Jeremy go play a game together while we get brunch on the table?"

"'Kay. Whatcha want to play, Jeremy?"

Jeremy shrugged. "Whatever." Not the nicest answer, Iggy thought. But did Jeremy get the fish-eye from his mom?

No. Jeremy's mom said, "Jeremy's got to eat like a horse this morning, because he has a recital this afternoon."

A recital. Of course. Because Jeremy Greerson played the cello. Jeremy Greerson was a reader. Jeremy Greerson had the best manners ever, said Iggy's own grandmother. Everyone old thought Jeremy Greerson was the most wonderful boy in the world. Even some kids thought that. Girls, mostly. But still.

The grown-ups went into the kitchen.

Maribel went with them (that was new too). Iggy and Jeremy looked at each other.

"Come on," said Iggy.

They walked toward the family room. When they got there, Jeremy looked around. "Where's your computer?"

Iggy did not feel like laughing at this point. "We don't have one in here."

"Where is it? Aren't we going to play a game? Do you have *Megalopolis*? I have *IX*, which is nine."

Iggy swallowed. "They don't let me."

"What?"

"They don't let me play computer games."

They did, actually, let Iggy play computer games. One hour a day, which he was *not* going to waste on Jeremy Greerson.

"Wow. Oka-a-a-y." Jeremy looked at Iggy in a certain way. The certain way was this: with pity for Iggy's sad, boring, dorky life and with joy for his own much better life. He had so much pity for Iggy that extra pity oozed out in his voice when he said, "What game do you want to play?"

At that moment, Iggy felt bad.

He felt even worse the next moment, when his little sister, Molly, came into the room. Molly

was three. Everything about Molly was round: her face, her eyeballs, her curls, and her stomach. She yelled at people a lot. She cracked Iggy up. Except not at that moment, because what she did when she came into the room was look at Jeremy, point her finger at Jeremy, and say, to Jeremy, "I like that boy!"

Jeremy laughed.

"Read me a book, boy!" said Molly.

Jeremy laughed again. "Okay."

Iggy couldn't believe it. Molly got a book and sat down next to Jeremy on the couch. She dug her elbow into his leg so he couldn't go away.

"Read, boy!" she said, and he did.

Those were things she did with Iggy, not with other people. Iggy sat down on the floor and pretended to do a puzzle.

In this way, time went by until enough had passed for Iggy's mom to call, "Brunch!"

CHAPTER 3

EXTENUATING CIRCUMSTANCES, PART ONE

This is a short chapter about a couple of long words. *Extenuating circumstances* are facts that make the things people do more understandable. They are pieces of information you need to know before you decide whether someone is good or bad. This idea is tricky, so here is an example:

1. A guy walks into a store and steals a loaf of bread.

2. A guy walks into a store and steals a loaf of bread because he hasn't eaten anything in two days.

Because he hasn't eaten anything in two days is an extenuating circumstance. Do you think it's less bad to steal the bread if you haven't eaten in two days?

I do.

Keep this in mind when you read the next chapter and especially when you read chapter six.

CHAPTER 4

THE SAME PANCAKE TWICE

Iggy felt better about Jeremy once he got to the table. He felt better about everything, because there was food. Tons of it, all things he liked, especially a giant pancake his mom only made on special occasions (which Iggy would not have called this).

"This is fantastic, Laurel," said Jeremy's mom, munching on her piece of pancake. "Jeremy is loving this pancake."

"Thanks. It's called a Dutch Baby," said Iggy's mom.

Dutch Baby?

Dutch Baby!

Iggy started to laugh. His mouth was full. You know what happened. Pancake everywhere. (By the way, this is not the bad thing that Iggy's going to do. This is not his fault in any way. Come on. Dutch Baby? It's just funny.)

But when he finally stopped laughing, everyone was looking at him like he was a worm and not just a worm, but a half-squashed, half-squirming worm.

Even Molly, who was all the time yelling and spitting her food out, held up her napkin to make a wall around

24

her plate. "That boy don't do that," she said, and pointed at Jeremy.

"I think you can be excused, Ig," said Iggy's dad.

Iggy looked at his plate. "But I'm not done."

(If only he had said "I'm sorry," everything would have turned out differently. But once again, not saying it cannot be called *bad*.)

"Oh yeah, you're done, kid," said his dad. "Outside."

"Iggy's *bad*," said Molly. (Incorrectly.)

Did Iggy push back his chair, scrape the floor, grab a sausage with his fingers, and stomp away, yelling "Good! I hate brunch anyway!"

No. He did not.

He only did the sausage part.

Out in his backyard, Iggy may have said "I hate brunch anyway!" and "Jeremy Greerson! What a [thing he was not supposed to say]!" Out in his backyard, Iggy may have kicked the picnic table. He may have turned red. He may have thrown a rock or two at the shed. He may have sat down with a thump and eaten his sausage and then wiped his greasy fingers on the chair. But so what?

After a while, to keep himself from thinking about Jeremy Greerson eating the pancake,

plus the sausages, the cheesy scrams, the tiny muffins, and the strawberries, Iggy took the net off the trampoline. Nets were for babies. Then Iggy lay down in the middle of the trampoline. He looked at the sky. He bounced a few times. If you keep yourself completely straight like a pencil and bounce, it's kind of fun. Not for very long, though. He hadn't even had a bite of his cheesy scrams.

Iggy got off the trampoline, found his skateboard, put it on the trampoline, sat on it, and bounced. It was a little more fun but not much more fun than being a pencil and bouncing. To cheer himself up, Iggy sang a song about pee. He sang it and bounced on his skateboard on the trampoline.

"What did you say?"

Jeremy Greerson was standing on the back porch.

Iggy knew that Jeremy Greerson would never sing a song about pee. Oh no, not him. He played the cello. He played the cello and had such nice manners, he was probably going to tell on Iggy.

"[Thing about pee]!" sang Iggy.

"I'd get killed if I sang that," said Jeremy. (This was not true. Jeremy might get a Talking-To, possibly a Reflection Time, maybe a Natural Consequence, but none of those was even close to being killed.)

"Oh yeah? My parents don't mind," said Iggy. (Also not true.) "They let me do what I want." (Extremely not true.)

Jeremy smiled his my-life-is-better-than-yours smile. "Like the computer?"

"Well." Iggy shrugged. "That, yeah, but they're okay with everything else."

Jeremy nodded. There was a silence. "What're you doing?" he asked.

Iggy did not want to say "I'm bouncing on my skateboard on the trampoline." That sounded stupid. Babyish. Pathetic. Instead, he said, "I'm pushing the trampoline next to the shed so I can skateboard off the roof and land on it."

Jeremy Greerson blinked. "That's insane."

Iggy shrugged again. "It's pretty fun."

"Let's see you do it," said Jeremy. What he meant was this: I don't believe you.

Iggy shrugged a third time. "Okay."

CHAPTER 5

A SHORT CHAPTER
ABOUT A SHORT BUILDING

This won't take long. I just need to say that the shed was short. Not nearly as tall as a house. The highest part of the roof was about eleven feet off the ground. If you can't picture eleven feet, it's about the height of two dads, one standing on the other's shoulders. That's how high the roof was. The roof was also not pointy. It wasn't flat, but it wasn't pointy either. It was a slope.

Got it?

Good.

Let's get back to business.

CHAPTER 6

THE ROOF

Do I need to tell how Iggy got out the ladder, how he climbed up the ladder to the roof of the shed, how Jeremy climbed halfway up the ladder to pass Iggy his skateboard, how Iggy looked down from the roof of the shed and suddenly noticed that the trampoline was extremely small, and how he said to himself, This is really going to hurt. Do I?

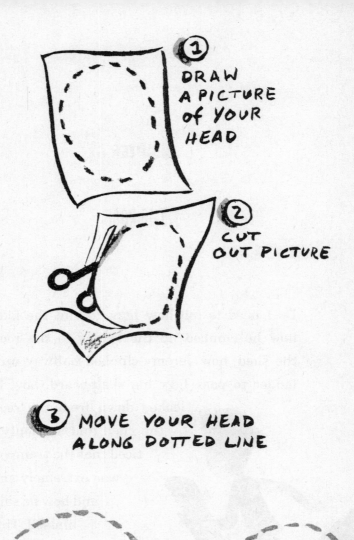

I think I can skip that part.

Because Iggy, good old Iggy, did it anyway.

I am sure you will be glad to learn that Iggy did *not* get hurt. This is because he did a really important thing with the skateboard as he was flying off the roof. I can't tell you what it was. Why? Because I have signed a contract promising that nothing in this book is dangerous. Every author has to sign this thing. Otherwise, our books don't get published. Of course, what Iggy did was *not* dangerous. It would have been dangerous if he hadn't done it. But if you read it and then tried to do it yourself, you would probably do it wrong, and your head would go bouncing around the lawn.

No! That was a joke.

Whew.

Let's get back to the story.

Iggy lay on his back on the trampoline, happy to be alive.

Jeremy, who was still halfway up the ladder, was looking down at him with his mouth hanging open. "I can't believe you did that."

"It was great," said Iggy. This was true, although the greatest part was still being alive. He looked at Jeremy's mouth-hanging-open face and added, "I do it all the time."

This was the first actual bad thing Iggy did. First, he was telling a lie, since he had never done it before and hoped never to do it again. Lying isn't good. But lying wasn't the very bad part. The very bad part was that Iggy said it to make himself seem cool and Jeremy seem not cool. This was not only bad, but also mean.

Plus it caused something else to happen.

"Let me try it," said Jeremy.

This was not what Iggy intended. Iggy intended to make Jeremy feel bad that he wasn't as brave as Iggy. It was a mean intention, but it wasn't a dangerous, head-bouncing-around-the-lawn intention. Jeremy skateboarding off the roof onto (if he were lucky) the trampoline? Yow. He'd never make it. He'd break his bones. He'd never play the cello again. And it would be all Iggy's fault.

"Nah. Better not," said Iggy. "You have that recital."

To Iggy's surprise, Jeremy's face got stubborn-looking. "I don't care. I want to."

Iggy thought fast. "You can't just do it. You've got to practice. Try jumping off the ladder first."

Jeremy's face was still stubborn. "But—"

"Try it," Iggy said.

So Jeremy did.

Some people might say "Oh, that Iggy is a terrible boy! He told Jeremy to jump off a ladder onto a trampoline." But those people would be wrong. Iggy was being a good boy, because jumping off a ladder onto a trampoline is a lot better than skateboarding off the roof of a shed onto a trampoline.

Also, it was fun. Jeremy had fun, jumping from the ladder to the trampoline. *Boing, boing, boing.* He loved it. You could even say that Iggy had been a good host by suggesting a fun thing for his guest to do. Really. You could say that.

After Jeremy had jumped six times from the middle rung of the ladder, he climbed up to the top rung. "Okay! Watch this!" he shouted, leaning forward for a dive.

The ladder wobbled.

"Hey!" yelled Iggy. "Don't do that!"

"What?" said Jeremy. He gave Iggy a try-to-stop-me face. Then he dived. And he landed right in the middle of the trampoline, safe and sound. He was laughing when he climbed off. "Cool! Now I'm going to do the roof."

"No! Don't. Really. It's super dangerous," said Iggy, grabbing the ladder to get it as far from Jeremy and the shed as possible.

"Give it!" said Jeremy, grabbing it back. He was stronger than Iggy expected (cellos are heavy). He yanked it out of Iggy's hands. "Like you could stop me anyway," Jeremy said. "You can't even keep food in your mouth." He set the ladder beside the shed and pretended he was spitting food. "It's like you're in preschool or something."

"Don't jump off the roof, Jeremy," said Iggy, ignoring Jeremy's extreme rudeness and trying to get close enough to pull the ladder away. "It's hecka dangerous, and you'll break something—" He put one hand on the ladder.

And Jeremy Greerson kicked him. "[Thing nobody is supposed to say]!"

"Hey!" Iggy fell over, holding his shin.

Jeremy made a snort-laugh and hurried up

the ladder to the roof of the shed. He
stood on the edge of the roof and made
the food-spitting face again. "Iggy the
Piggy!" he called.

Iggy forgot how much his shin hurt.
He forgot that and everything else.

"Is that your real name,
Iggy the Piggy?"

Iggy was on his feet.

"Think you can stop me?" Jeremy
gave a giant pig snort.

Iggy was tearing up the ladder.

"Dream on, Iggy-Piggy."

Iggy was screeching, "You're
dead, Jeremy Greerson!"

And at this moment, all
three parents came outside
to see what the boys were
doing.

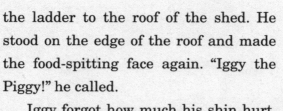

CHAPTER 7

WHAT THE PARENTS SAW

Here, in order, is what the parents saw:

1. Jeremy standing on the edge of the roof of the shed
2. Iggy storming up the ladder, screeching, "You're dead, Jeremy Greerson!"
3. Jeremy looking over his shoulder in terror as Iggy reached the roof
4. Iggy lunging for Jeremy
5. Jeremy leaping wildly into the air, screaming, *"Helllllp!"*

CHAPTER 8

THE UNDEAD

Jeremy didn't die. This is a children's book. Kids never die in children's books.

No. Wait. There is one where a kid dies.

I hate that book. I would never write a book like that. So. No need to worry. Jeremy is not dead.

Now you're probably guessing he broke his arm.

Wrong! He didn't break his arm either.

In fact—he was fine. Certainly he was *scared*, as anyone would be if he plunged through the air and boinged off the trampoline and slammed into the ground. But he was fine. He even played at his recital that afternoon. It wasn't his best performance ever, but maybe he hadn't practiced enough.

I want to say it one more time: Jeremy Greerson was one hundred percent A-okay!

Think about that.

Here is some time for you to think:

. . .

. . .

Now think about what you know about *extenuating circumstances*. If necessary, go back and look at chapter three.

. . .

. . .

Now think about Iggy.

Iggy, who had been called Iggy the Piggy plus a thing that nobody is supposed to say plus being sent outside for accidental spitting plus not getting foods he liked plus being smiled at in a pitying way plus being kicked. Think about all that.

Now look back to the last chapter, to the list of what the parents saw.

. . .

. . .

Put all of these ideas together, and I think you'll agree with me that the big problem was timing.

The big problem was all three parents coming out on the back porch at the exact moment that Iggy was rushing up the ladder screaming "You're dead, Jeremy Greerson," and Jeremy made the choice—the *choice*—to leap from the roof. It looked bad. It looked as though Iggy had chased Jeremy off the roof.

But here is an important point: What seemed to be happening was *not* happening. Iggy had

been trying to stop Jeremy from jumping off
the roof. If Iggy had caught Jeremy on the roof,
he might have hit him, but he would not have
pushed him off the roof. Jumping off the roof had
been Jeremy's own idea. Iggy hadn't made him
do it.

Iggy did his best to make this clear to the
parents.

They didn't believe him.

Jeremy stood next to his mom, still a little pale and sweaty, not saying much. He could have helped Iggy by telling the truth, but he didn't. However, he also didn't mention the thing that Iggy had done with the skateboard. If he had, Iggy's parents would have given him one of their famous make-him-regret-it-so-much-he'll-never-do-it-again punishments. Iggy was almost grateful that Jeremy said nothing.

Of course, there were some bad minutes. There was a minute with Dad pointing his finger at Iggy's face. A minute with his mom looking sad. An even worse minute when there were tears sparkling in her eyes. (But after that, she hugged him and whispered that she just wanted him to think for once in his life, think!) There was a series of bad minutes when the punishment was being explained.

Then the door to Iggy's room closed behind his dad.

Iggy heard his mom and dad whispering in the hall. He didn't feel good. How could he? His parents thought he was terrible. They were probably wishing they had a son like Jeremy

Greerson. He could almost hear them say "If only Iggy were like Jeremy, we would be so happy."

Was that what they were saying?

He pressed his ear against the door, but all he heard was "Rrrmm-uh!" from his dad and "Ss-huh, ruh-suh" from his mom.

Then their shoes on the stairs.

Then it was quiet.

Iggy lay on his old, hairy rug. He felt bad.

If I could do it over, thought Iggy, I wouldn't chase Jeremy up the ladder, and I wouldn't yell "You're dead, Jeremy Greerson." I wouldn't try to make Jeremy feel uncool either.

Wow! That punishment was working!

Then Iggy thought of Jeremy's face when he'd seen Iggy reach the roof. He thought of Jeremy's expression when he realized that Iggy was going to hit him. He thought of the precise moment when Jeremy decided that it would be better to jump off the roof. And in that tiny fraction of a second, Iggy could see that Jeremy Greerson regretted everything he'd done that had led to this moment.

Iggy smiled. "Oh, yah!" he whispered. "I play the cello!" His smile grew bigger. "I have *Megalopolis IX*. That's nine, you know."

Iggy snickered. He rolled over and buried his face in the rug so no one would hear him. And then he laughed and laughed and laughed.

He laughed until he was tired. That was great, he thought. Too bad I got in trouble.

CHAPTER 9

WHERE IGGY WENT

Do you remember the first chapter of this book? You do not! You're a big faker. Just go back and read it.

. . .

. . .

Hurry up!

. . .

. . .

This chapter is about Number 2: Things we wish we hadn't done quite as much as we did. Things that weren't ever a good idea, but wouldn't have been bad if we hadn't gone too far. That's what this chapter is about. In this chapter, Iggy goes too far.

It began one day after school. Most afternoons, Iggy hung out with Diego or Aidan or Arch or somebody else he liked. Or he had soccer. Or he went with his mom to pick up Molly or take Maribel to dance class.

But on this day, his mom had a meeting.

Maribel and her friend Haley were going to walk Iggy home from school and watch him for two hours until his mom got home. Iggy didn't like it. What did "watch" mean? Did it mean

they were going to tell him what to do? They'd better not! Maribel was only two and half years older than he was! And Haley! The day Haley got her new cell phone, she'd dropped it in the toilet! What gave her the right to watch him? Nothing!

Walking home from school, Iggy decided that he wouldn't let Maribel and Haley boss him around.

They might think they were in charge of him, but they weren't. They might think they could ruin his afternoon, but they couldn't. He'd show them!

Actually, though, Maribel and Haley didn't try to ruin Iggy's afternoon. In fact, they seemed to be completely uninterested in Iggy or his afternoon.

Iggy took three cookies for snack. Maribel didn't say "You know you're only supposed to have two."

She said, "Do you want me to pour you some milk, Ig?"

"I can pour my own milk," said Iggy firmly.

"Okay," said Maribel.

He spilled a little.

After his snack, Iggy said, "I'm going to play *MonsterTrack!*" Maribel didn't say "You know you're not supposed to play computer games in the afternoon."

She said, "Okay." Then she said, "Ooh, Haley, look at this cute shirt!"

Iggy played *MonsterTrack*. He played for an hour and ten minutes. He was only supposed to play on the computer for an hour, but nobody stopped him. He kept looking at the clock. Nine minutes. Ten minutes. Where were they? Iggy got up. He went to listen in the hallway.

"So then she said, Kylie, you can't wear those, it's against the rules, and then—" Maribel paused. "Iggy, stop listening!"

"I'm not!"

"Go away, or I'll tell Mom you bugged us."

What? "You call that watching me?" Iggy yelled. "I could be dead for all you know!"

"Go away!"

Iggy stomped as hard as he could into the nearest room, which was the bathroom, and slammed the door. He locked it too. *Click*. So ha. If they didn't want him around, he'd stay in the bathroom! And when they had to pee, he wouldn't let them in. So ha!

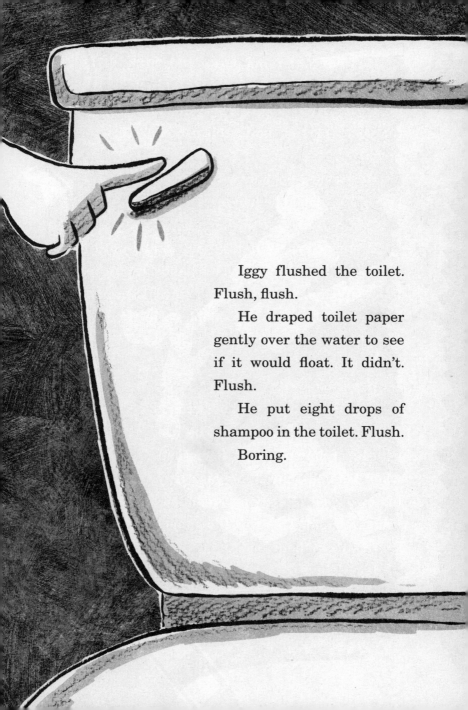

Iggy flushed the toilet. Flush, flush.

He draped toilet paper gently over the water to see if it would float. It didn't. Flush.

He put eight drops of shampoo in the toilet. Flush.

Boring.

He went to the sink part of the bathroom. He turned Maribel's toothbrush upside down so the brush part was touching the yucky part of the toothbrush cup. So ha!

He brushed his hair with Maribel's brush. He wished he had lice.

(Not really.)

He turned the water on and waited until it got warm. Then he washed his hands. He turned the soap around and around until his hands foamed with millions of bubbles. He tried putting some on his chin, for a beard.

It dripped off.

It was too watery.

Shaving cream would be better.

His dad wouldn't care if he used a little bit of shaving cream. Sometimes, when his dad shaved, he gave Iggy his own glop of shaving cream to smear around. This was the same thing, only without Dad.

Iggy found the shaving cream. He shook it, the way he'd seen his dad do. Then he sprayed.

Wow. That stuff really flew.

He wiped it off the wall and put it on his face, patting it into a beard shape.

He laughed. So this was what he was going to look like when he was an old guy.

Better put on a mustache too.

(This was when Iggy began to lose his mind.)

And just a little bit in his hair. To make it white.

(Did he ever think, Maybe I shouldn't? Nope. He didn't.)

He needed more, to make it really white. Yeah. That was it. All over.

(It was like he forgot there would be life after that minute.)

Iggy looked in the mirror at his white beard and white mustache and white hair. He still looked like a kid. He needed wrinkles. He opened his mom's makeup drawer. Yeah! The stuff she put on her eyes. Eyeliner. Cool. He gave himself a lot of wrinkles.

"Arrrrr," he mumbled, like an old guy.

(Iggy's mom's car pulled into the driveway.)

"Arrrr," he groaned. He was really old.

"Iggy?" called Maribel, outside the door. "Are you okay?"

"Arrrr-rrr," gasped Iggy softly.

"Iggy! Did you hurt yourself?"

What a great idea! Blood! And here was all the lipstick in the world, just waiting for him!

(It was like his brain had gone on vacation.)

Iggy drew a trail of blood down the side of his face. It seemed small. More like a trickle. He didn't want to wreck the wrinkles or the white hair. But it was a shame not to be bloodier. Arms! Iggy pushed up his sleeve and drew an enormous gush of blood on his arm. Whoa! It looked like someone had tried to cut his arm off! Chop! He drew a big circle of blood around his neck. Someone had tried to cut off his head! Fun! Too bad the top of the lipstick snapped off. He could have done his stomach!

"Aggggggggggggggh!" he moaned, staggering around the bathroom. "They got me!"

"I'm home, kids!" called Iggy's mom, coming in the front door.

"Mom!" shouted Maribel. "I think Iggy's hurt! He's in the bathroom crying, and I can't get in!"

(Most of Iggy's brain was on vacation. The only part still at work was the hand-moving part. Because what Iggy did then was flip the lock on the bathroom door, fling it open, and jump out into the hall covered in shaving cream, eyeliner, and lipstick.)

"AGGGGGHHHH!" he bellowed.

CHAPTER 10

EXTENUATING CIRCUMSTANCES, PART TWO

Actually, there are zero extenuating circumstances in that bad thing. At least, I can't think of any. It wasn't as if anyone had locked Iggy in the bathroom. It wasn't as if Maribel and Haley were giving Iggy a hard time or bossing him. No. The truth is Iggy was bored and lonely, so he went into the bathroom, and while he was there, he lost his mind.

However, I would like to point out that he didn't do anything terrible. Anything *amazingly* terrible, that is. It was not so good that Maribel cried. But she only cried for a minute or two. It definitely wasn't good that his mom dropped her coffee cup when he jumped out of the bathroom. But there was hardly anything in it.

The worst thing was the lipstick. The lipstick was ruined. His mom was pretty upset about that. She wasn't happy about the eyeliner either, but it wasn't ruined. There was just less of it. The lipstick was bad. Iggy had to buy a whole new one with his own money. Iggy figured lipstick would cost the same as a marker, but it cost thirteen dollars! That was when Iggy wished a lot that he hadn't gone too far.

But was this terrible?

Really terrible?

I don't think so.

Here are two reasons why:

TWO REASONS WHY THIS WAS NOT TERRIBLE

1.   Ruining lipstick (or eyeliner) isn't
     life-threatening. Wearing that stuff is
     probably bad for you anyway.

2. Sometimes when people lose their minds, they do way worse things than Iggy did. Like for instance, they write with lipstick on the walls. You know who I'm talking about. At least Iggy didn't do that.

Unfortunately, neither of these is an extenuating circumstance.

CHAPTER 11

PUTTZI

Yes. You're right. We're here. This is the chapter about Number 3.

Remember Number 3? The thing we really, completely wish we hadn't done.

The thing we feel really bad about. The thing we wish we had never thought of.

Why is this chapter called Puttzi?

Because I'm the author, that's why.

What is Puttzi?

Puttzi is Iggy's fourth-grade teacher. Of course, he didn't call her Puttzi. Not to her face, anyway. He called her Ms. Schulberger. She was his favorite teacher ever. She was young and pretty and nice. She wore necklaces with different funny things on them, like a tiny hammer or fractions. She didn't call Sharing Sharing; she called it Gossip, and you could tell stuff you weren't supposed to know as long as it didn't hurt anyone's feelings. Instead of one class pet, her class had three, four if you counted crickets. For Global Studies, she spun the globe and wherever your finger stopped, that was where you were going to live when you grew up, so you had to learn three words in its language, and she didn't get mad if two of them were *Bathroom! Quick!*

Ms. Schulberger never got mad. All of Iggy's other teachers had gotten mad. His second-grade teacher, Ms. Dixson, had been mad most of the year. She had sent Iggy to the principal so many times that the principal got mad too. "Not again, Iggy!" she'd yelled. Even the school secretary got mad. "I am tired of seeing your face, Iggy Frangi," she'd said. It had hurt Iggy's feelings.

Ms. Schulberger never hurt his feelings.

Every morning, she said "Iggy!" like she was happy to see him. When he painted his buttons during art, she didn't get mad. She said they looked nice. The closest she ever got to being mad was when he licked the fish. And even then, she said, "If you're hungry, tell me, and I'll give you a snack."

Iggy loved Ms. Schulberger. He never would have said it out loud, but he did. Out loud he said "She's pretty nice." If he was with Arch or Owen or Skyler, he said "Puttzi's a nutzi." As long as she didn't hear it, it wasn't bad.

Ms. Schulberger was called Puttzi because of her car. She had the tiniest car in the world, a putt-putt car. It looked like an oven with tires. It was so tiny that one time, he and Arch and Owen had almost picked it up. They couldn't quite, but almost. If Skyler had been there, they would have.

Secretly Iggy was glad Skyler wasn't there. Skyler was mean. He might have helped them pick it up, but he also would have made them do something else to it, like drop it on its side. Iggy didn't want to do that to Ms. Schulberger or her tiny putt-putt car.

But one Monday—

One Monday—

Can we take a break here?

Thank you.

WORLD'S GREATEST DESK
LID
STORAGE
SEAT
SIDE
SEAT
DESK SURFACE
TOP

CHAPTER 13

THE NEW OLD DESKS

Okay. Let's do it.

One Monday, the fourth graders came in to find Ms. Schulberger's classroom had changed. Over the weekend, their two-kid tables had been replaced with separate desks for each kid. And these weren't just any desks. These were special big-kid desks with the chair part connected to the table part. And a lift-up top, so you could put your stuff inside and keep it secret. The new desks were arranged around the classroom in two U-shaped rows.

Ms. Schulberger explained that their tables had been needed at another school. Their new desks, she said, were actually very old. They would be getting brand-new ones very soon. In the meantime, they would have to make do with these old desks. "I'm sorry about that, kids," said Ms. Schulberger.

Iggy and Arch exchanged looks. What was she talking about? These desks were fantastic. They were the best desks Iggy had ever seen.

Ms. Schulberger read them the schedule, and they began the regular Monday-morning things, including Weekend Reports by Sarah and Arden. Girls' weekends were so boring Iggy wondered how they could stand it. He couldn't even stand hearing about it. He lifted up his lift-up top; he could probably fit the class snake in there. He looked at Arch. Arch was putting his

head inside his desk. That was good. Iggy put his head inside his desk too.

"Iggy and Arch. Please listen to Arden!" said Ms. Schulberger.

Okay. Iggy listened. Arden was going to be a flower girl at her cousin's wedding. Molly had been a flower girl a few months ago. "Aren't you too old to be flower girl?" yelled Iggy. "Aren't you supposed to be, like, three?"

"Iggy! Do I need to move your name?" said Ms. Schulberger.

Iggy was surprised. Moving his name meant taking his name tag off Yellow, where everyone was at the beginning of the day, and putting it down to Orange or—no!—even Red. It meant he had done something bad. But what? Was it the yelling?

"Sorry!" he yelled.

Ms. Schulberger sighed.

Okay, if she didn't want him to talk, he wouldn't. Arden's dress had ribbons on it. Big whoop. He looked over at Arch and rolled his eyes. Arch rolled his eyes back. Iggy slumped (quietly!) in his chair and grabbed his throat. Arch hung his tongue out of his mouth. Iggy went stiff, like he had been electrocuted. Arch pretended to fall out of his chair. Then he almost fell out of his chair for real.

But Iggy didn't notice that last bit, because he had just noticed something else.

When Iggy went stiff and pushed his back against his desk chair with all his weight, the front of the desk rose off the floor.

Huh.

Interesting.

What would happen if . . .

Iggy put his arms under the desk. Okay, good. He could reach. He cradled the bottom of the desk in his arms, kind of like he was holding a baby. Then, slowly, he leaned back. The desk lifted up, so that the only thing touching the floor was the chair-leg part. And of course his feet.

He walked forward, driving the desk.

Arch burst out laughing, and Ms. Schulberger looked up.

"Iggy!" she snapped. Ms. Schulberger, who never snapped. "Come and sit in front where I can see you! Right now. You too, Arch. I can't believe it's only nine twelve and I'm moving your names to Orange. Honestly!"

Iggy blushed. He had to sit in front? Like Skyler? Skyler had to sit in front because he had cut off part of Anaya's dress. That was really bad. Iggy hadn't done anything like that. How unfair.

He and Arch exchanged looks. He could see that Arch thought it was unfair too.

Skyler laughed.

CHAPTER 14

A LUNCH MEETING

Diego was Iggy's best friend. After kindergarten, the school had made a rule that Iggy and Diego could never be in the same class again. The school couldn't stop them from hanging together at lunch, though.

At lunch, Iggy told Diego all about the new old desks, particularly about the way you could drive them if you wanted to. Diego said that was hecka cool and wished he had them in his class.

Arch was sitting nearby. So was Skyler. So was Owen, who was also in Iggy's class.

Iggy and Arch and Owen and Diego and—
sort of—Skyler were famous. They were not famous for being good. Or for being helpful and
polite. Or for playing the cello or reading or
painting watercolors.

To be honest, they were famous for getting
in trouble.

Of course, they were famous for other things
too. Arch was famous for an unbelievably terrible thing that had once happened to him when
he went camping. I can't tell you what it was.
Owen was famous for drawing. Iggy was famous
for being a fast runner and really good at soccer
and for almost falling into a baboon pit. Diego
was famous for being really good at soccer and

for building things like go-karts with his dad. Skyler wasn't famous, or if he was, it was for all the stuff that he was probably going to do when he was older, like go to jail.

"Ig and Arch got in trouble for it," said Owen. (Remember? They were talking about desk driving.) "Puttzi got mad and moved them to Orange."

Iggy felt this was an unnecessary piece of information to give Diego. "Puttzi's jealous," he said. "'Cause her car's smaller than my desk." He nodded to himself. "If we raced, I'd win."

"You'd kill," said Arch. (By kill, he meant win. Of course.)

Iggy smiled now. "We should have a desk race. When she's not looking."

Skyler, who may or may not have had a toothpick in his mouth, said, "Puttzi can be the finish line."

"Yeah!" Iggy said, laughing. "We can all charge her at once! Like she turns to do something on the board, and we all go right then. *Bbrrrrrmmmm!*"

"She'd freak!" said Owen enthusiastically.

"We'd get moved to Red," warned Arch.

"Who cares?" said Skyler. "It'll be fun. Iggy and I'll do it, at least. I'll beat you, Ig."

"No you won't," said Iggy. "You'll probably wipe out, knowing you."

"Psh. Bet I won't," said Skyler.

"Bet you will," said Iggy.

(Did you notice what just happened? If you count up only thirteen lines, charging at Ms. Schulberger with their desks was a funny idea. Now it's a plan.)

"I bet on Iggy," said Diego, a loyal friend.

"I bet on me," said Arch.

"Loser," said Skyler. He leaned forward. "Okay, so here's what we do . . ."

CHAPTER 15

BUNDLE UP

It was hard to concentrate that afternoon. Luckily, Iggy didn't have to concentrate much in math. Math was pretty easy. Bundling, which Ms. Schulberger was teaching that afternoon, was especially easy. Ones, tens, hundreds. Ten ones is the same as one ten. Ten tens is the same as one hundred. What's not to get?

Something, apparently. Because a lot of people didn't get it. Some people (like Donal!) never got anything, but even people (like Anaya!) who normally got everything didn't get bundling.

"Let's think about money, people," said Ms. Schulberger. She turned to the whiteboard.

Iggy tensed, but it was only the second time she'd turned. The third time was the starting flag.

Ms. Schulberger faced the class. "When we had ten pennies, we exchanged them for one dime. Right?" She nodded hopefully. "Now, looking at our place-value columns, if you have ten dimes, what can you exchange them for?"

"A hundred pennies!" said Anaya.

Which was true, but not what Ms. Schulberger wanted to hear. Iggy knew what she wanted to hear: Ten dimes are the same as one dollar. Normally, he would have raised his hand, but he couldn't raise his hand because he had to keep his arms under his desk so he could start desk racing the instant she turned for the third time.

He glanced at Skyler, who was looking at him. Loser, mouthed Skyler.

He glanced at Owen, who was leaning back in his chair. Owen would never win. He was slow.

He glanced at Arch. Arch looked back at him and nodded like, I'm going to beat you.

". . . also the same as one hundred," Ms. Schulberger was saying. "So, look, if I *bundle* my tens into groups of ten, what do they become?" She whirled around to the whiteboard to draw bundles.

"Three!" said Skyler.

"PUTTZI!!" yelled Owen, Arch, and Iggy, zooming forward in their desks. Skyler didn't yell. He just zoomed.

Ms. Schulberger turned around to see four desks blasting toward her at warp speed.

Iggy charged as fast as he could. He was laughing and driving and making car-squealing sounds. So he only glimpsed Ms. Schulberger's face in the very last second before he reached her.

And in that very last second, Iggy thought . . .

This was

a bad idea.

Ms. Schulberger screamed.

CHAPTER 16

BAD, BAD, BAD

"I'm sorry," Iggy said for the fiftieth or sixtieth or ninetieth time. He swallowed. "I'm really, really sorry."

He was saying it to the school secretary. Why the school secretary? Because the principal was in Ms. Schulberger's class, teaching it. Because Ms. Schulberger had to go home. Because Iggy had (a) run into her knee and (b) scared her and (c) made her cry.

Iggy felt terrible. He had never felt as terrible as he did then. He cried, he felt so terrible. When Ms. Schulberger screamed and he bashed into her because he couldn't stop and then Owen (who came in second, surprisingly) had crashed into him, making him bash into Ms. Schulberger again, and she had fallen over holding her knee, he had cried. He had started apologizing then, but no one could understand him because he was crying. Also because no one could hear him over all the yelling.

After a minute of everyone yelling, Arden and Cecily ran to get the principal and after that—Iggy couldn't stand thinking about it— three firefighters came in with their big first aid cases and even—no!—even a stretcher, and then the biggest firefighter said, "How did this happen?" and Lainey, who was the nicest girl in the class, looked at Iggy with hatred and pointed her finger and said, "He did it."

"I'm sorry!" Iggy cried.

"You should be," said the biggest firefighter.

Iggy groaned, thinking about it.

And then Iggy was sent to the office, along with Arch and Owen, who were sort of crying, and Skyler, who had never cried in his entire life. Walking there, Iggy was embarrassed that he was crying so much, and a year later, he was more embarrassed about crying in front of everyone than he was about crashing into Puttzi. But ten years later, he thought that crying was probably the only reason he wasn't expelled from fourth grade.

CHAPTER 17

WHAT HAPPENED TO IGGY ONCE HE GOT HOME

I don't want to talk about it. All I'm going to say is this: It took a year.

CHAPTER 18

THE END

This is not the end of the book. It's only the end of Number 3: The thing we wish we had not done at all.

Neither Ms. Schulberger nor Iggy went to school the next day. Ms. Schulberger, because she was resting her knee. Iggy, because he was suspended.

The day after that, Iggy went back. He wished he didn't have to. He thought about running away to Ketchum, Idaho. Then he thought about his mom and decided not to. He went to school, and everyone looked at him hatingly except for Arch and Owen and Diego, who looked at him sympathetically. And Skyler, who looked at him the way he always did, like he'd never seen him before in his life.

But Ms. Schulberger wasn't there. She was still resting her knee.

Iggy thought the worst was over.

Iggy was wrong.

The worst was the next day, when Ms. Schulberger came back. She came back with Mr. Schulberger, who was even bigger than the big firefighter and had a long blond ponytail and a beard. He helped Ms. Schulberger into a chair and squeezed her arm. Then he said, "Which one is he?" Ms. Schulberger smiled and shook her head at him.

"Which one of you is Iggy?" asked Mr. Schulberger.

Iggy didn't raise his hand, but everyone else helpfully pointed at him.

Mr. Schulberger marched like a big blond giant across the classroom to Iggy. He leaned down and said, very softly, in Iggy's ear, "Don't ever do that again."

"I'm sorry!" said Iggy.

"You should be," said Mr. Schulberger, just like the firefighter.

"Jack!" said Ms. Schulberger. "Good-bye." She waved at him. He went away.

I'm sorry.
I'm sorry.
I'm sorry.
I'm sorry.
I'm sorry.
I'm sorry,
I'm sorry.
I'm sorry.
I'm sorry.
I'm sorry,
I'm sorry.
I'm sorry.
I'm sorry,
I'm sorry.
I'm sorry,
I'm sorry.
I'm sorry.
I'm sorry,
I'm sorry.
I'm sorry,
I'm sorry.

Iggy didn't make a sound all morning. He kept his eyes down and his hands to himself. It almost killed him. When the recess bell went, he jumped to his feet, wanting like crazy to tear out of the room.

But he didn't. He waited until all the other kids had gone out. Except Arden, who was a kiss-up and always stayed inside until Ms. Schulberger made her leave.

"Off you go, Arden," said Ms. Schulberger. "Iggy and I are having a talk."

Arden trailed away, looking hatingly over her shoulder at Iggy.

"I'm sorry," said Iggy.

Ms. Schulberger nodded.

Iggy opened his lift-top desk and took out the things he had brought. The first was a drawing he had made. It was very embarrassing. It was a flower.

Below the flower, it said "Get Well Soon" and "I'm sorry." The second was a letter. In it, he had written "I'm sorry" a hundred times. Then an equal sign. Then "I'm sorry" in ten groups of ten. He had circled each group and written "bundling" on the side, in case she didn't get it. The third thing was a bag containing two candy bars he had bought with his own money, plus some other candy left over from Halloween.

He gave all these things to Ms. Schulberger.

"I'm sorry," he said.

"Why did you do it, Iggy?" she asked.

"What? The race? I don't know."

Ms. Schulberger said nothing, and Iggy thought maybe he should try to explain it better. "I thought it would be funny."

I'm sorry.
I'm sorry.
I'm sorry.
I'm sorry.
I'm sorry.
I'm sorry.
I'm sorry.
I'm sorry.
I'm sorry.
I'm sorry.

I'm sorry.
I'm sorry.
I'm sorry.
I'm sorry.
I'm sorry.
I'm sorry.
I'm sorry.
I'm sorry.
I'm sorry.
I'm sorry.

Ms. Schulberger looked up quickly.

"Not to hit you!" Iggy said. "That wasn't what I thought was going to happen. We were just using you for the finish line. I didn't think we'd hit you."

"Of course you were going to hit me. You were aiming for me. But really, Iggy, my question is *why* were you aiming for me? I thought we got along."

"We do! We aimed for you because— because—" Iggy couldn't remember why. "I don't know. I just thought it would be fun."

Her eyes got narrow. "What's Puttzi?"

"You," muttered Iggy.

"Why?"

Iggy looked up in astonishment. How could she not know? "Because of your car! It's a putt-putt car."

Ms. Schulberger blinked at him. Then she smiled. "Oh, Iggy. You're a nut."

Iggy laughed. "So are you! Sometimes we call you Puttzi the Nutzi!"

"Don't call me that!"

"I'm sorry!" he said quickly. But she was smiling. "I wish I hadn't banged into you," he said.

"Me too," she said, rubbing her knee.

"I'm going to try hecka hard not to do anything bad for the rest of the year," said Iggy.

"That would be nice," she said.

"I probably won't make it," he said.

He didn't make it.

CHAPTER 19

EXTENUATING CIRCUMSTANCES, PART THREE

Officially, extenuating circumstances are things that happen *before* the person does the bad thing. They are pieces of information that explain *why* someone did the bad thing.

So officially, there are no extenuating circumstances for Iggy's desk-racing incident. Ms. Schulberger moving him to Orange doesn't count. It's nothing at all like not eating for two days.

Iggy was the one who discovered desk driving. Iggy was the one who suggested charging Ms. Schulberger when her back was turned. Iggy was the one who called it a race.

Why did he do those things? Not even Iggy could tell you why. All he could say was: I thought it would be funny.

That is not an extenuating circumstance.

But unofficially, I think we can say that Iggy's sorriness *became* an extenuating circumstance. He felt so bad about what he had done that he actually made it better.

Of course, this wouldn't have been extenuating if he had broken Ms. Schulberger's kneecap.

But her knee was okay by the next week.

And he drew her a picture of a flower.

And he wrote "I'm sorry" two hundred times, in bundles.

All of this made Ms. Schulberger know that Iggy was really, truly sorry.

Even years later, when Iggy thought of the moment Ms. Schulberger turned and saw him and screamed, he felt bad. That's how sorry he was.

That's extenuating, isn't it?

I hope so.

CHAPTER 20

THE REAL END

Look! You read a twenty-chapter
book! What a good kid you are.
Not as good as Jeremy Greerson,
though. You can just forget
about that.

TURN THE PAGE FOR A SNEAK PEEK
AT THE NEXT BOOK IN
THE IGGY SERIES!

CHAPTER 1

WHAT THIS BOOK
ISN'T ABOUT

You know those books where the main kid becomes a better person at the end? You should. You've read about a million of them.

For example, the main kid excludes another kid, and then the other kid wins some big thing like a race and becomes really popular, and then the main kid feels left out, and from this, he learns to be nice and not to exclude anyone ever again. The end.

Sometimes, the main kid is already okay at

the beginning of the book, but he gets even better by the end. Say, the main kid *kills* at basketball, but by the end of the book, he learns that people who play the flute are just as good as people who kill at basketball. The end.

The main kid can also learn a rule, like Don't Light Stuff on Fire. Or he can learn to keep on trying even when the going gets tough. It can be anything. The point is for the main kid to be better at the end than he was at the beginning.

Would you like to know why there are so many books about becoming a better person?

Because grown-ups like it when kids get better. They think it's nice.

And they're right. It *is* nice.

Unfortunately, in this book, nobody gets any better.

Sorry.

Nobody gets any worse, though!

So that's good.

Iggy (that's the main kid, also known as the *hero*, of this book) stays pretty much the same all the way through. He learns a few things, but they aren't things that make him better. They are things about gardening supplies.

But mostly, Iggy gets in trouble. He does Thing 1, and then Thing 2 happens, and then, unfortunately, Thing 3 happens too. Does he learn from the bad things he does? Does he say to himself, Whew, that was really bad. I have learned my lesson. I'm going to stop doing that bad thing and become a better person!

No. He doesn't.

Some people think that kids will learn their lesson if they experience a terrible consequence when they do something wrong. For example, if you're not supposed to climb on the roof, but you do it anyway and then fall off and break your leg, this will teach you never to climb on the roof again. This is the whole idea behind punishments.

3

Punishments were invented for the times when you climb on the roof, but you don't end up with a broken leg. Grown-ups worry that you won't learn your lesson if there's no terrible consequence, so they make one up. That's what a punishment is.

Does Iggy get punished for doing his bad things?

He sure does!

Do his punishments make him wish he hadn't done them?

Not exactly.

To tell the truth, Iggy would do them all over again in a second.

Now, you are probably feeling kind of bad yourself because you're reading a book about a kid who doesn't get better. You're probably saying to yourself, Gosh, I wish I were reading a book about a kid who plants flowers by the side of the road instead of this book about Iggy getting in a bunch of trouble! If that's how you're feeling, I have some good news for you. Even though Iggy doesn't get any better during this book, *you* will. By reading about the bad things Iggy does, you will learn not to do those things, and that will make you a better person. Isn't that great?

To help you become a better person, I am going to include special notes after each bad thing Iggy does to remind you that (a) boy, was that bad! and (b) don't do that! I'll even put the notes in big type so you can show them to your grown-up and say, "Look! Reading this book is making me a better person!" The big type will also make it easy for you to skip those parts if you don't want to read them.

But enough about you! Let's get to the bad things Iggy does. Like most bad things, it began on a . . .

CHAPTER 2

MONDAY

Here's Iggy on Monday morning. Yup, that's him.
That's his bowl of cereal. That's his dad. That's
his big sister, Maribel. His little sister is still
asleep.

Why is his head on the table?

Don't you ever put your head on the table?

No?

Well, aren't you polite.

Iggy looks like he's asleep, but he's not. He's thinking. He's thinking about how much he doesn't want to go to school.

"Eat your breakfast, Ig," says his dad.

"I don't want to go to school," Iggy says. Actually, he yells it.

But does anyone pay attention? No.

Maribel says, "I need a new backpack."

His mom, who isn't in this picture because she's in the next room looking at her computer, says something about how terrible the traffic is.

Then his dad says something else about how terrible the traffic is.

(Have you ever noticed how much time grown-ups spend talking about traffic?)

Iggy moans a little.

Does anyone feel sorry for him? No.

"We all have problems, Ig. Stop moaning and eat your breakfast," says his dad.

Guess what! You can eat breakfast and moan at the same time!

"Stop that. You like school," says Iggy's dad. "Remember last week you said Ms. Schulberger was your favorite teacher ever."

This is totally unfair. Ms. Schulberger *is* Iggy's favorite teacher ever, but liking your teacher isn't the same as liking school. He would probably like Ms. Schulberger even more if he only saw her once a month. Plus, he's only had four other teachers, so how can he know for sure she's his favorite? Maybe next year, in fifth grade, he'll have a teacher he likes better than Ms. Schulberger. He says this.

"Ha," says Maribel. She's eleven, so she's in middle school, but she used to go to Iggy's school. "You'll have either Ms. Keets or Miss Hackerman, and you better hope you get Miss Hackerman, because Ms. Keets will kill you."

Iggy frowns. Why would she kill him?

Maribel leans over her cereal and whispers, "In my year, there was this kid who fell out of his chair by mistake, and Ms. Keets cut his hat."

"Whaddaya mean, cut his hat?" whispers Iggy.

"In the paper cutter," says Maribel. "He fell out of his chair by *mistake*. So think what Ms. Keets would do to you."

Iggy thinks. He thinks about all the times he's fallen out of his chair on purpose. Sometimes he yells "Whooo!" when he does it. Sometimes he pretends to trip when he's going to the whiteboard. Sometimes—hardly ever—he slides under the table and ties other kids' shoelaces together so they fall over when they stand up.

Ms. Keets probably *would* kill him.

"What about Miss Hackerman?" Hackerman! It sounds like she would kill him too.

Maribel shrugs. "Miss Hackerman's nice. She wouldn't kill you, because she likes everyone. But she's old. She could be gone by next year. She was sick for something like a month when I had her. And guess who our substitute was."

"Who?"

"Mrs. Wander." Maribel grins at Iggy and makes a chopping motion across her throat. "*Ha-ack!*" she chokes.

Is Maribel choking on her cereal? No. She isn't. What is she doing, then? And why?

Let me explain . . .

CHAPTER 3

A SHORT CHAPTER
ABOUT
A SHORT PERSON

Mrs. Wander is the principal at Iggy's school. She is very short. She's so short that most fifth graders and even some fourth graders are taller than she is. There's nothing wrong with being short. Plenty of people are short and funny. Plenty of people are short and friendly. But Mrs. Wander is not these things.

Mrs. Wander is short and scary.

When kids see Mrs. Wander coming, they stand completely still, hoping her eyes will slide over them. Mrs. Wander doesn't like kids who move. She especially doesn't like kids who run.

Running, she says, is not safe. Mrs. Wander is crazy about safety. She loves it. In Iggy's opinion, it isn't very safe to be so scary that you almost make kids pass out when they see you. But nobody's asked Iggy's opinion.

Here's another thing about Mrs. Wander: She doesn't like Iggy very much.

Actually, she doesn't seem to like him at all.

They have spent a lot of time together, especially the year Iggy was in second grade. That year, he was sent to her office so many times, he had his own chair. Mrs. Wander even put a sign with his name on it on the chair. Iggy thought that was mean.

Sometimes people like you more when they get to know you. Not Mrs. Wander. The more she got to know Iggy, the less she liked him. When Mrs. Wander saw Iggy, her eyeballs would bulge

with fury, even if he was standing completely still (which, to be honest, he usually wasn't).

So what would happen if Mrs. Wander were his teacher?

Iggy would have to run away to Ketchum, Idaho.

TURN THE PAGE TO READ ABOUT
IGGY'S OTHER BOOKS!

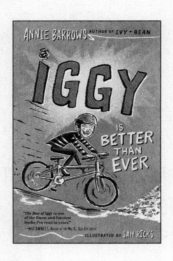

ONE THING LED TO ANOTHER . . .

Have you ever heard those words? Sometimes it means "Things got better." That's not what it means in this book.

In this book, Iggy gets an idea—a perfectly fine idea—and then, unfortunately, the principal shows up, and then, even more unfortunately, there's an incident with a basketball, and then, before you know it, Iggy is flying through the air.

How did it all happen? It's really hard to explain. You'd better read the book.

HERO OF EVERYTHING?
IT DEPENDS WHO YOU ASK . . .

From Iggy's point of view, his house-protection plan was genius, pure genius. From Iggy's point of view, he saved (a) his candy, (b) his family, and (c) the toaster. From Iggy's point of view, he should get a trophy. And respect.

And more candy.

So what if Rudy Heckie disagrees? Rudy Heckie has been wrong before, and he'll be wrong again. Rudy has a scar now, and scars are cool! He should be happy. So should Mr. Heckie. So should Iggy's mom and dad. Everyone should be happy. Specifically, everyone should be happy with Iggy.

But are they? It all depends on your point of view.

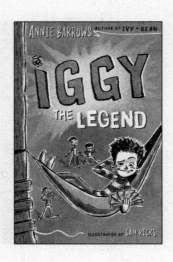

GROWN-UPS ARE ALWAYS CHANGING THE RULES!

When grown-ups make money, it's good. But when Iggy makes money, all of a sudden it's bad.

When grown-ups find something interesting on the sidewalk, it's finders keepers. But when Iggy finds something (very) interesting, finders keepers turns into You're In Trouble.

Why is Iggy being blamed for something they never said he couldn't do?

What did he do, you ask?

Something legendary!

DON'T WORRY—
MORE OF IGGY'S TRIUMPHS ARE ON THE WAY!

NOW AVAILABLE WHEREVER AUDIOBOOKS ARE SOLD